Nuts About You
Coloring Pages

Hillary A. Hinds

Nuts About You

Coloring Pages

ISBN: 978-1-7771012-0-6

Written by Hillary A. Hinds, Books4dNations Learning Innovations.

Cover and book illustrations by StallionStudios88

Published by Hillary A. Hinds, Books4dNations Learning Innovations

Cataloguing in Publication may be obtained through Library and Archives Canada

To the Nations' Kids

Love

Hillary

Find the
Nuts

Find the Squirrels

Drawing Page

Drawing Page

Drawing Page

Drawing Page

Drawing Page

Drawing Page

About the Author

Hillary A. Hinds is the author of the children's books, *Rabbit Goes to Church*, *Blessings from Above*, *Mama Bear Knows Best,* and *It's My Time* inspirational journal. She was born in Jamaica and currently resides in Canada.

Hillary is the founder of Books4NAtionsKids of Saskatchewan, which provides faith-based books to kids and different charities worldwide.